THE BOY AND THE AIRPLANE

MARK PETT

SIMON & SCHUSTER BOOKS FOR YOUNG READERS
New York London Toronto Sydney New Delhi

pat
pat
pat

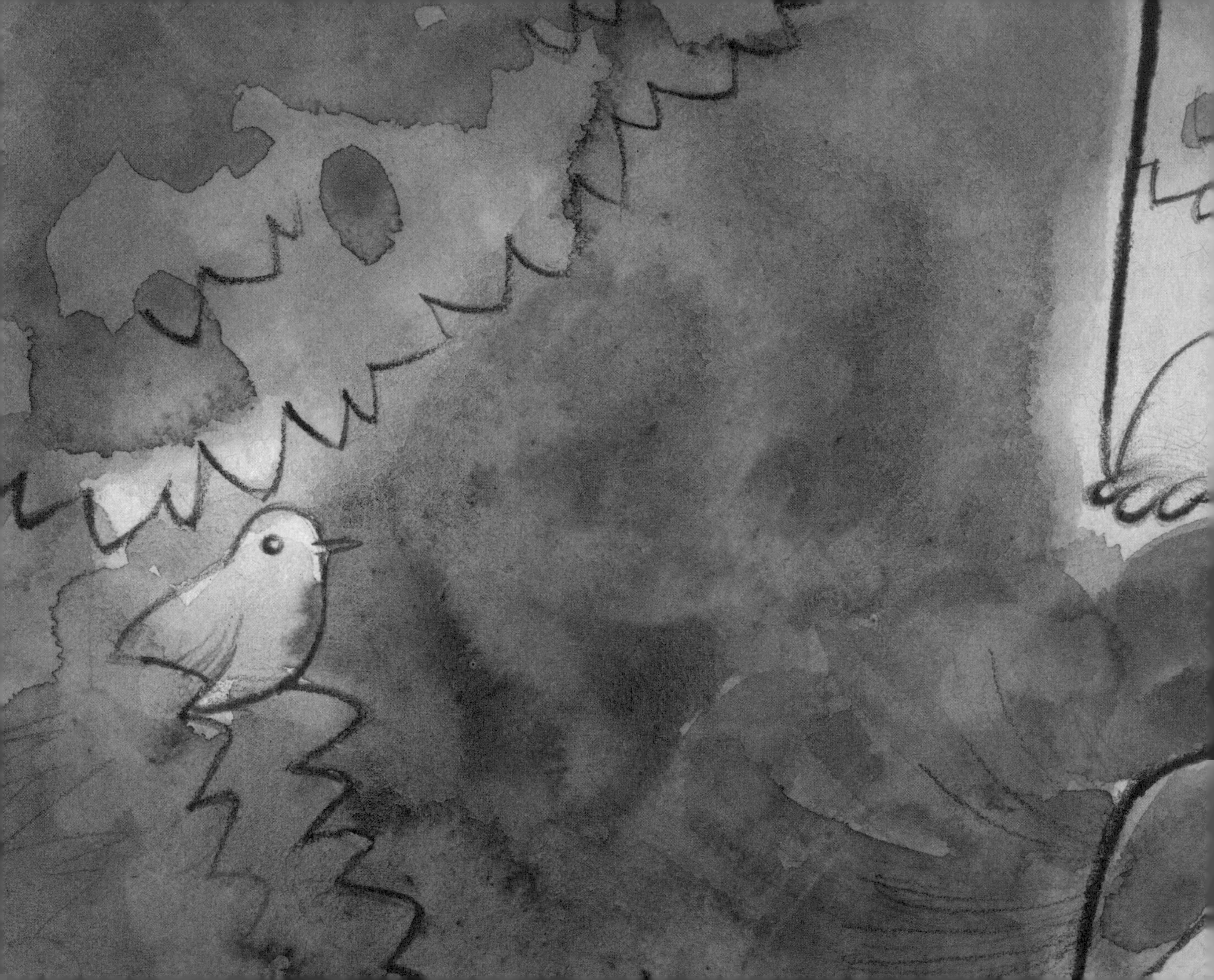

FOR TIFFANY, WHO WAS WORTH THE WAIT

SIMON & SCHUSTER BOOKS FOR YOUNG READERS
An imprint of Simon & Schuster Children's Publishing Division
1230 Avenue of the Americas, New York, New York 10020

For information about special discounts for bulk purchases, please contact Simon & Schuster Special Sales at 1-866-506-1949 or business@simonandschuster.com.
The Simon & Schuster Speakers Bureau can bring authors to your live event. For more information or to book an event, contact the Simon & Schuster Speakers Bureau at 1-866-248-3049 or visit our website at www.simonspeakers.com.
Book design by Lucy Ruth Cummins
The illustrations for this book are rendered in pencil and watercolor.
Manufactured in China
0113 SCP
2 4 6 8 10 9 7 5 3 1
Library of Congress Cataloging-in-Publication Data
Pett, Mark.
The boy and the airplane / Mark Pett.—1st ed.
p. cm.
Summary: A wordless picture book in which a boy comes up with an inventive solution for getting his toy airplane down from the roof.
ISBN 978-1-4424-5123-0 (hardcover)
ISBN 978-1-4424-5125-4 (eBook)
[1. Lost and found possessions—Fiction. 2. Toys—Fiction. 3. Stories without words.] I. Title. II. Title: Boy and the airplane.
PZ7.P4478Boy 2013
[E]—dc23
2011040935